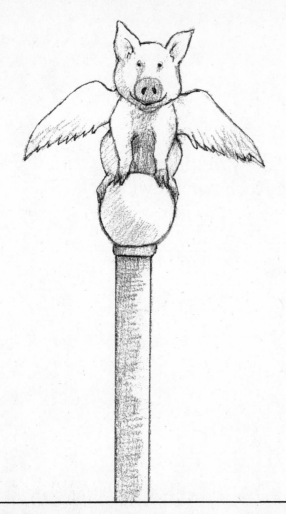

PERFECT THE PIG

by Susan Jeschke

Scholastic Inc.
New York Toronto London Auckland Sydney

To my mother,
Victoria Kochman Newmark

ISBN 0-590-43710-0

12 11 10 9   4/9

He was so small that his mother didn't know
he was there. The other piglets were always
pushing and shoving, squealing greedily for food.

But the tiny pig was gentle, quiet, and never greedy.
He always kept clean. While the other piglets rolled
around in the mud, he would lie under his favorite
tree wishing for wings to carry him into the sky.

One day he heard a terrible squeal. A large sow
had fallen in the road. The little pig crawled
under the fence and ran to help her.

He had to push with all his might, but at last he got the sow up on her feet again.

The sow thanked the little pig, and she offered him
a wish. "Anything at all," she said.
"I want wings," he answered.
The sow nodded and went on her way.
Almost at once wings began to grow on the little pig.

He was thrilled! His wings worked!
He flew around all day.

At night he went back to the pigpen. When the
other pigs saw his wings, they pushed him out.
"Go sleep with the birds," they said.

But the birds wouldn't let him stay either.

On and on he flew until he came to a big city.

He landed on a fire escape, too tired and hungry
to go on. A woman came to the window.
"So tiny, and with such beautiful wings!"
She took him inside.

The woman fed the little pig, then put him to bed
and kissed him good night. The little pig
kissed her back. "How perfect!" the woman said.
And she named the little pig "Perfect."

Perfect could hardly believe it. He had not only
found a home, but also someone who thought
he was perfect.

The woman's name was Olive. She loved Perfect
and did all she could to please him.
She gave him baths . . .

. . . and fed him the very best vegetables from the plants she grew in her apartment.

Olive was an artist. She liked to paint pictures
of Perfect sitting among the fruits and vegetables.
He was a wonderful model.

However, Perfect soon grew restless.
He began to look longingly at the sky —
he missed flying.
Olive understood and took him up to the roof.

He flew about while she waited for him. From then on,
he went out flying for a short time every day.

Olive took Perfect out on walks, too.
She made a little jacket to cover his wings
so he wouldn't attract attention.
But Perfect didn't like walking. The hard cement
hurt his feet, and he couldn't see anything.
So Olive carried him in her basket.

She did her best to hide the bad things
in life from him, but she didn't always succeed.

Whole Pigs
ALL SIZES

People liked the paintings of Perfect
and bought them from Olive.
Her savings jar began to fill up.

Soon Olive's apartment became crowded with fruits
and vegetables and a growing Perfect. He had grown
so much that he was getting too big to hide.

Olive decided that the best thing for both of them
would be to live in the country. She made a label
for her savings jar. It said, HOUSE IN THE COUNTRY.
Perfect couldn't read, but he could see that Olive
was very happy and excited. That made him
happy and excited, too.

But their happiness did not last long. The next day,
while Perfect was out flying, a heavy fog rolled in.
Perfect got lost. He flew around all day looking
for home, but he couldn't see a thing.

When the fog lifted, Perfect spotted a park bench.
He landed on it and fell sound asleep.
A man's voice woke him. "Well, I'll be —" the man
said. "A pig with wings! My fortune is made!"

He picked up Perfect and ran home with him.

Perfect found himself in a small room. The man took off his belt and said, "Okay, Oink. Now I'm going to train you. Fly around this room!"
He cracked the belt like a whip, and Perfect flew away from it in fright.
"That's a good Oink," the man said.

Then he poured out some garbage and gave it
to Perfect to eat. Perfect was shocked.
He ran to the window and tried to get away.

"Oh, no you don't," the man said, and he tied Perfect to a pipe.

When the man thought he had trained Perfect enough,
he dressed him in a costume and took him
to a park to perform.

At the end of the show, Perfect flew over the audience. Everyone *oohed* and *ahhed*, and they gave the man lots of money. Perfect had to do the same thing every day.

Every night the man counted his money, then tied
Perfect up even tighter. "You're not going to get
away from me, you flying pork chop," he said. But he
was still worried that Perfect might somehow get free.

So the man bought a cage and locked Perfect up.

Perfect was miserable. His wings ached, and he hadn't had a bath in months. The man gave him nothing but garbage to eat and never, ever, kissed him.

Every night Perfect cried himself to sleep thinking of Olive.

Olive went up to the roof each day and searched the sky for Perfect. She walked through the streets looking for him everywhere.

Sometimes she wondered if Perfect had been
a dream. But she still had one painting of him.
It reminded her that he was real.

One day when Olive was out walking she saw
a sign that read, THE GREAT FLYING OINK.
She bought a ticket and ran into the theater.

She could hardly believe her eyes. It was Perfect!

The man was leaning over him saying, "Fly, you stupid Oink — or it's off to the butcher with you!" But Perfect couldn't budge. He was too sad, and his wings hurt.

"Perfect!" Olive cried out. Perfect raised his
head. He squealed happily as he stretched his
wings and flew to her. Everyone clapped.

Olive took off the rope that was tied around Perfect's neck.
"Where are you going with my pig, lady?" the man said.
"This is *my* pig," said Olive.
She and the man began to argue.
"Let a judge decide this," someone said.

The judge listened to both sides. Then he said,
"I think the pig should choose!" And of course,
Perfect chose Olive. The judge told the man to
give Olive half the money he made with Perfect.
It was Perfect's rightful share, he said.

Olive took the money and bought a little house
in the country, where she and Perfect lived in
peace and happiness.